When Solomon Was King

by Sheila MacGill-Callahan

pictures by Stephen T. Johnson

Dial Books for Young Readers

New York

Published by Dial Books for Young Readers
A Division of Penguin Books USA Inc.
375 Hudson Street
New York, New York 10014

Designed by Atha Tehon
Printed in Hong Kong
First Edition
1 3 5 7 9 10 8 6 4 2

Library of Congress Cataloging in Publication Data
MacGill-Callahan, Sheila.
When Solomon was king / by Sheila MacGill-Callahan;
pictures by Stephen T. Johnson. — 1st ed.
p.   cm.
Summary: As he grows more and more powerful,
King Solomon forgets the lesson he learned from a wounded lioness.
ISBN 0-8037-1589-7 (trade). — ISBN 0-8037-1590-0 (library)
1. Solomon, King of Israel — Legends. [1. Solomon, King of Israel. 2. Folklore, Jewish.]
I. Johnson, Stephen T., 1964–   ill.   II. Title.
PZ8.1.M1715Wh   1995   398.22 — dc20   [E]   93-28058   CIP   AC

The full-color artwork was prepared with watercolors and pastels.
It was then color-separated and reproduced as red, blue, yellow, and black halftones.

Author's Note:
In Jewish folklore it was said that King Solomon's ring enabled him to talk
with animals. I used that idea as a springboard in creating this story.
S. M-C.

For my sisters, Christine MacGill and Patricia MacGill McGowan
S. M-C.

For my sister Anne
S. T. J.

In the days when King David sat upon the throne of Israel, he called his son, Prince Solomon, to him.

"My son," he said, "you are now old enough to help get food for the palace. You will go with my huntsmen and you will obey them in all things, unless their commands touch upon the royal honor."

Solomon was overjoyed at this sign of becoming a man. For several days they hunted but had no luck. Now, because it was the eve of the Sabbath, they were returning to the palace, even though they were empty-handed.

The sun was slanting to the west when Solomon saw a wounded lioness lying beside the trail. One of the hunters prepared to loose his spear, but pity stirred Solomon's heart and he stayed the man's hand.

"It offends the king's honor to slay a helpless beast, Reuben. And she can be healed, so there is no need to put her out of her misery."

So saying, he dismounted and crouched over the lioness who had been wounded by an earlier hunter's spear. The head of the spear was still caught in her shoulder and her eyes were dull with pain and fever. Along her belly her teats were swollen with milk.

"Return to the palace," he commanded. "Tell my father that I will keep the Sabbath here in the wilderness in the service of life."

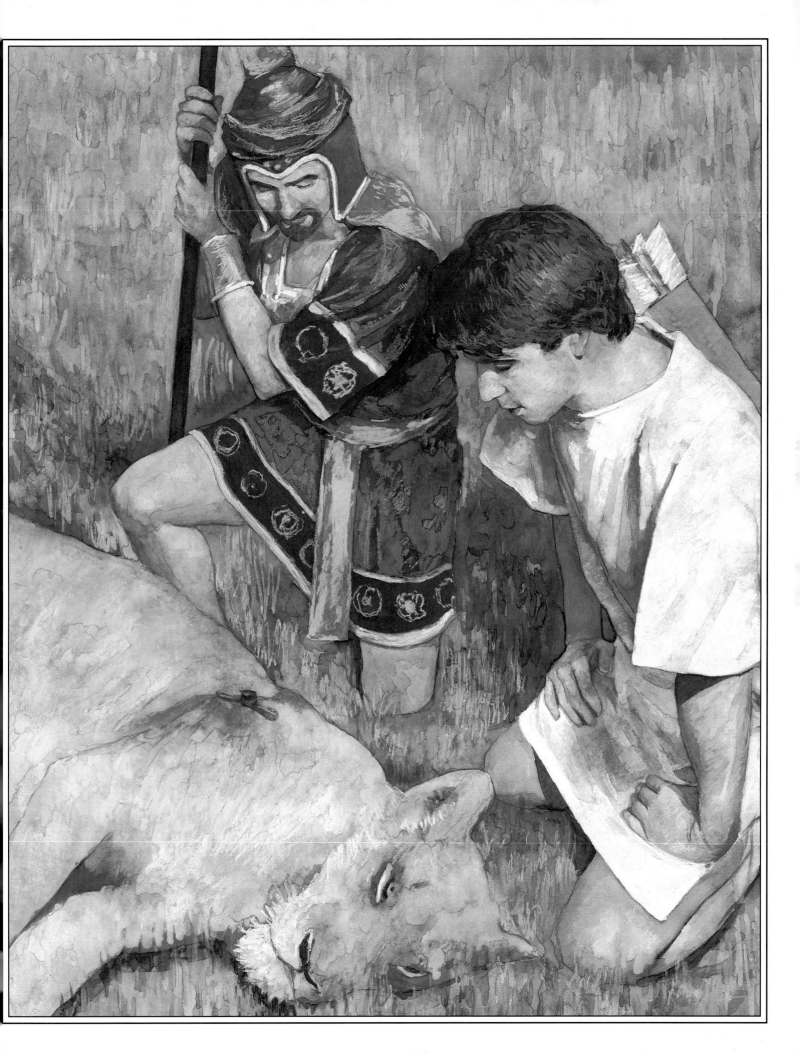

Understanding seemed to flare in the lioness's eyes. She waited patiently as he loaded his horse with food, wine, and oil, then she turned away from him and struggled painfully through a wide cleft in the rocks.

Solomon followed. She led him to a wide meadow where two cubs cried pitifully from hunger. Solomon gently pushed the babies away from their mother and fed them himself with scraps of meat and sweet water from a nearby spring.

At sundown he lit the Sabbath lights to honor the God of Israel. By their fitful gleam he drew out the spearhead and bound up the lioness's wound, pouring in wine and oil. That night he sat by her side, cooling her fever with water from the spring. By morning her eyes had cleared and her cubs were busily nuzzling for milk.

Because travel was forbidden on the Sabbath, Solomon passed
the day in prayer and in study of the wonders of the earth in
the hidden meadow. He lay upon his stomach and marveled at a
colony of ants who went about their lives, never knowing that
a being too large for their eyes to see watched their every move.
He traced the flight of the bees from clover patch to their hive
in a hollow tree. He listened to the birds' songs.

The meadow grass was sleeked silver by moonlight when he
mounted his horse for the homeward journey.

The years passed. King David was called to his reward in Abraham's bosom and Solomon became the king. He received great gifts at his crowning. One of them was a ring that gave him the power to rule the animals and speak with them in their own tongues. He ruled with justice and mercy, protecting the weak, fearsome to the wicked, and his fame went out to the far corners of the earth.

As time went on, Solomon forgot that his power was a gift. He grew proud and decided that his mastery and knowledge came from his own virtue; that he could do what he wanted, and that he would never die. His people started to tremble before him.

One day he and his men were out hunting. They had taken no game and were angry and tired. Not an animal stirred in the countryside, except a great eagle who flew above, uttering sharp cries as the hunters approached.

By the power of his ring Solomon knew the eagle was warning the other animals to flee. He called sharply to her in her own tongue.

"Why do you ruin the pleasure of your king?"

The eagle plummeted like a stone to land upon his saddlebow. "Because, great king, you hunt for pleasure and it is not worthy of you."

Solomon's pride was stung, as was his curiosity. "How can you say this? Do I not have power over all the animals?"

"I say it because your storehouses are full of grain and your fields with flocks. The power was not given to you for pleasure. Follow me." The eagle rose once more into the sky. Solomon looked around, but all his men had disappeared. He and his horse were on a different trail near a cleft in the rocks. Somehow it looked familiar. Over his head the eagle flew above the cleft. He followed. When he emerged, memory returned — he was a boy again with pity in his heart for a wounded lioness. But he did not have time to dwell on his memories.

A terrible roar was followed by the sound of rushing feet as a huge lion came charging across the meadow. Solomon stood frozen with fear, too terrified to invoke the power of his magic ring. Time slowed, each second seemed an hour as his doom approached.

Then the lion was upon him, his cruel claws unsheathed and raised to strike. The words he had whispered so often into the ears of the dying, *"Know, O Israel, the Lord thy God, the Lord is One,"* rose unbidden to his lips, when he heard a howl rise up from a nearby cave.

The lion sheathed his claws, but still held Solomon tight against the ground as an ancient lioness came slowly into the light. Her muzzle was gray and her eyes nearly blind. On her shoulder was a long-healed scar.

"Stop, stop, my son. It is the boy grown to a man. The one who saved my life and yours when I was wounded and left for dead by the cruel hunter."

"Are you sure, Mother," answered the lion, "that it is not your age and your longing to see the youth again to thank him that deceives you into thinking this is the man? For this man is a hunter. See the arrows and spears upon his horse."

"I am he," said Solomon, whose courage had returned and so he could draw upon the power of his ring. He knelt on the ground to caress her head and explained to her son, "I am Solomon, King of Israel. It was your mother who taught me about love and courage, by her love for you and your sister when you were little, and her bravery in seeking help from the same kind who had wounded her and left her for dead. And it was here on your meadow that I marveled at the diligence of the bee and the ant. And it was here that I learned true music from the songs of the birds."

"Why, then," asked the lion, "do you now come armed and unattended against a fellow king?"

"I was brought here by the eagle who sees all things, to be instructed and humbled. For in my pride I forgot the source of my power. Come back with me to Jerusalem, and live in my palace as my honored guests."

"No," said the lion, "it cannot be. For I am King of the Beasts and have my duty, just as the Queen Bee has hers and cannot leave the hive, and the Queen Ant hers and cannot leave the anthill. But we will come from time to time and visit." And with that Solomon had to be satisfied.

The lions kept their promise and people marveled to see them
walking at ease around the palace, conversing as equals with the king.
And the people of Israel never again hunted for pleasure.